Blue's Clues

Good Night, Blue

by Angela C. Santomero
illustrated by Jenine Pontillo

Simon Spotlight/Nick Jr.

Hi out there! Can you see me? It's me, Steve! Are you in your pajamas? Blue and I are *so* excited to have you sleep over at our house!

Blue, our pajama party guest is here! Oh . . . I think we need to whisper. Sidetable Drawer is asleep already.

Okay, Blue, what's one of the first things we do when we get ready to go to bed?

Brush our teeth! You're right!
Squeeze, brush, and rinse!

First we squeeze toothpaste onto our toothbrush. Great! Then we brush our teeth! Don't forget our back teeth! Then we rinse our mouth. So clean! What's next?

Wash our face! Exactly! Don't forget to use soap and water when you wash your face—and get behind your ears, too! Then we need to dry off with a towel.

Aaah! That feels nice and clean, doesn't it? So, Blue, what should we do next?

Go to the bathroom! Exactly. We don't want to have to get up in the middle of the night!

And don't forget to wash your hands! Now, what do we need to do next?

Get our pajamas and slippers on! Blue's favorite pj's are her blue dotted ones. What are your favorite pj's?

Now we are all comfy and cozy.
What should we do next?

Sing a bedtime song! What song do you sing at bedtime? Really? Okay, so . . . sing that song! I'll listen.

Wow. That was a great song! Okay, so how about a bedtime story? Wait a second—I think we just read a bedtime story!

Do you know what we should do next?

Go to sleep! Good night, Blue!
And good night to you, too!
Happy dreaming!